# BIG
# &
# JUMBO
## ILLUSTRATIONS

## Coloring Book For Toddler

## BELONGS TO:

..........................

by

Island Colors

If your child likes this coloring book please leave a review.

Thank you -)

ISLAND COLORS

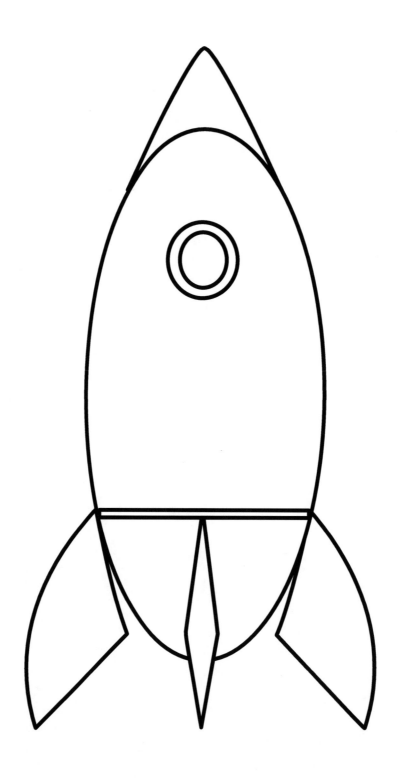

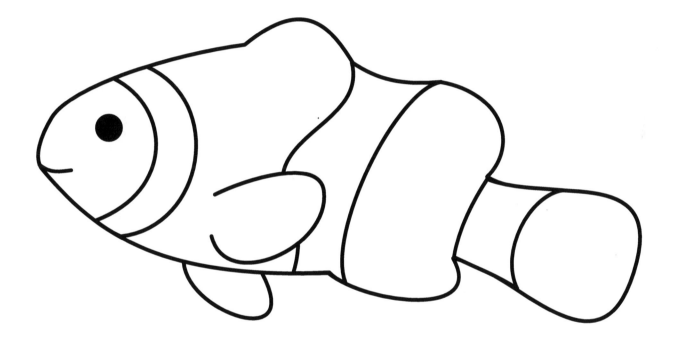

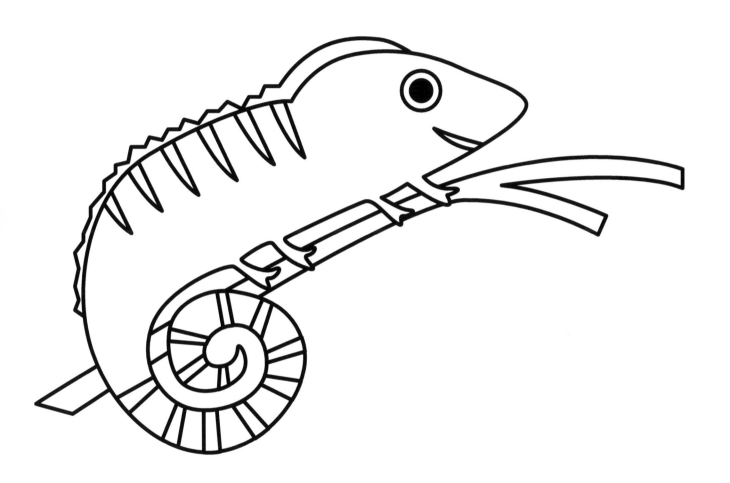

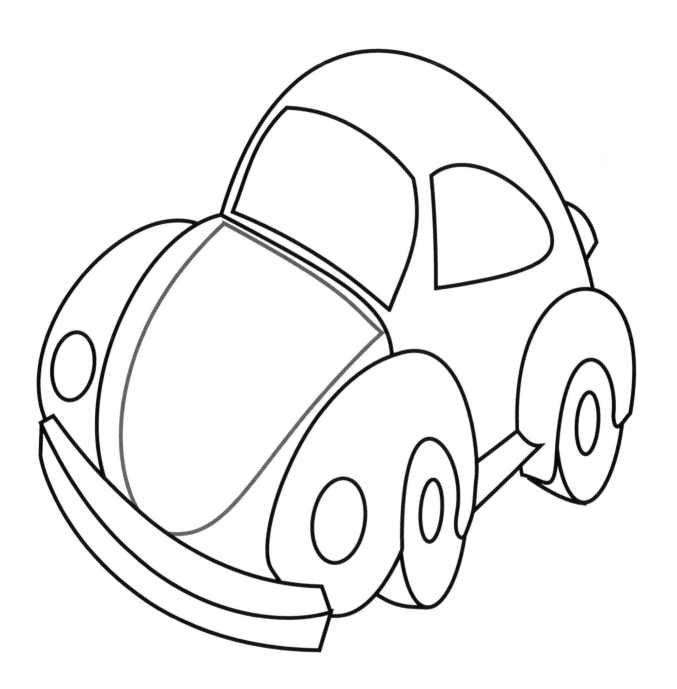

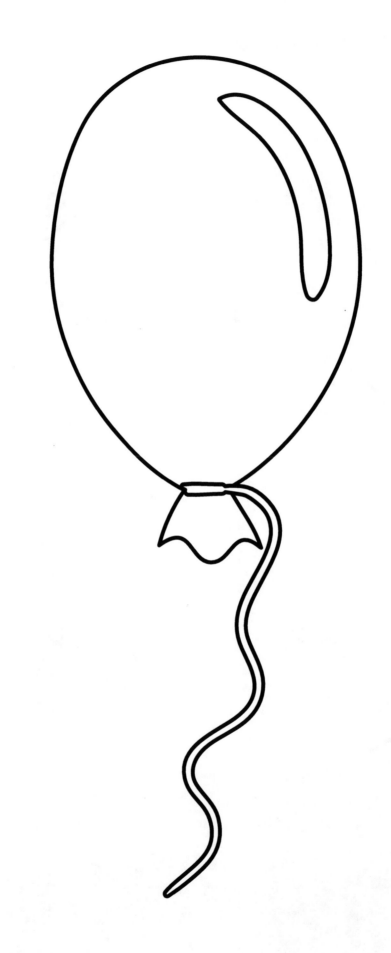

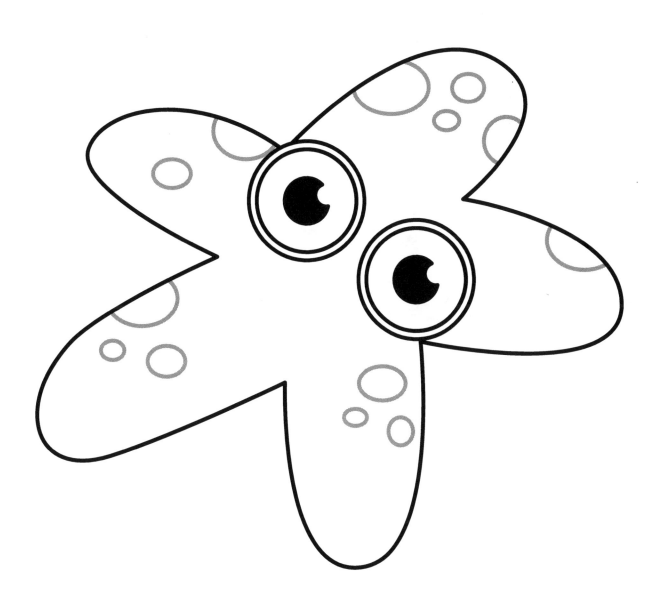

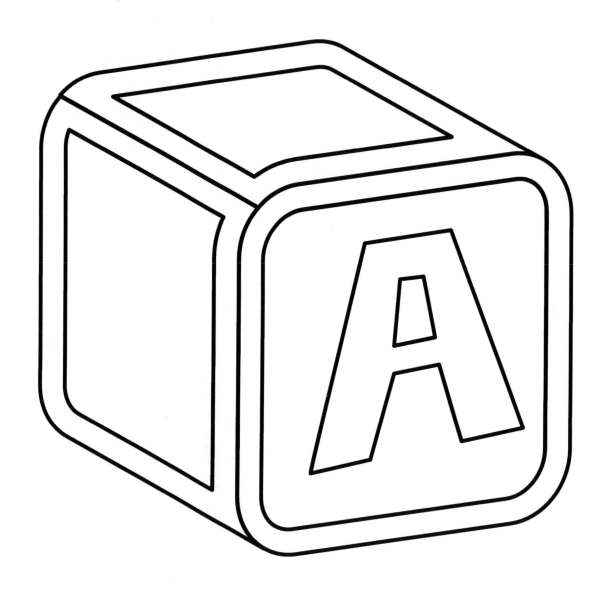

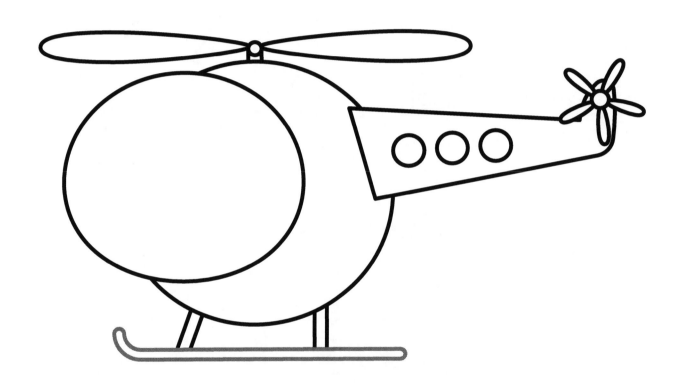

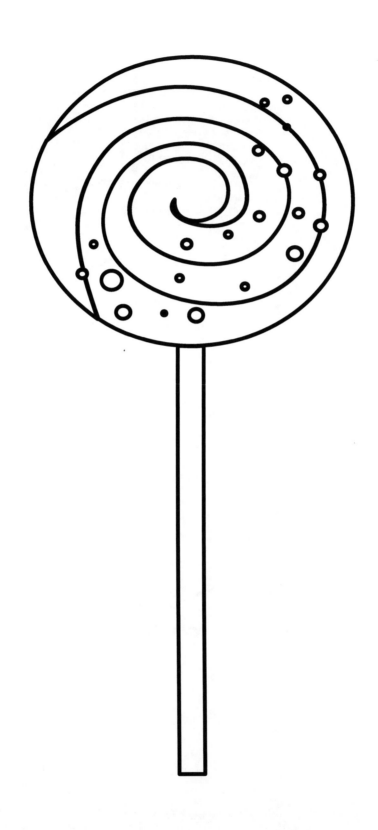

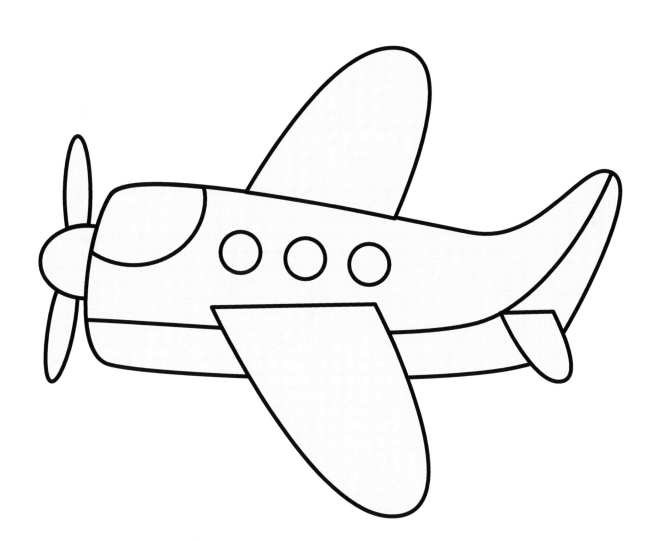

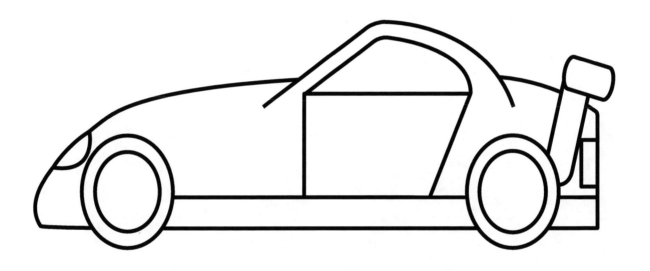

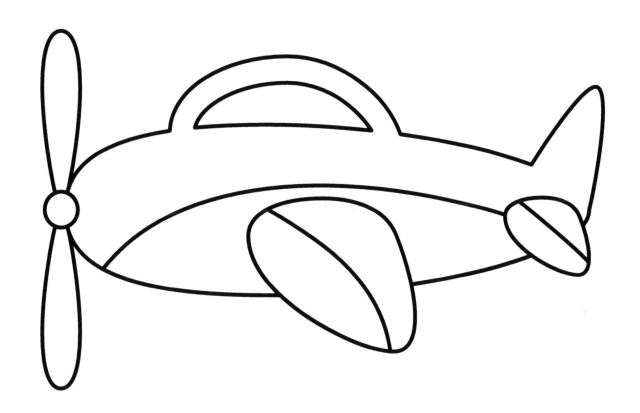

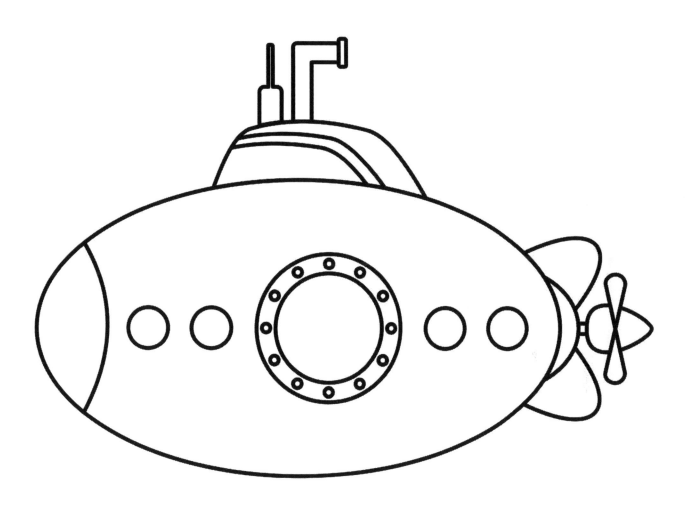

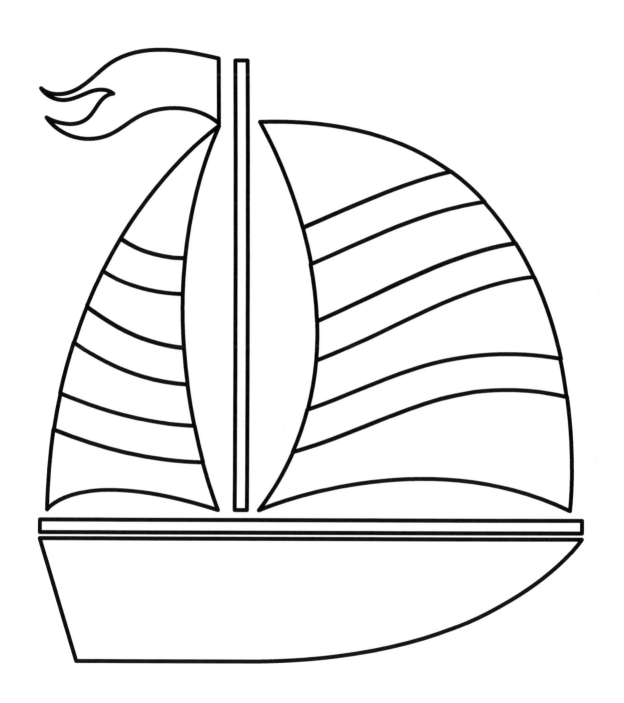

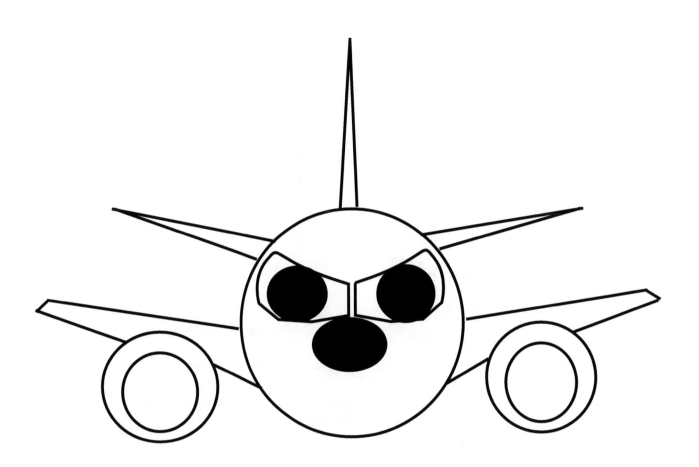

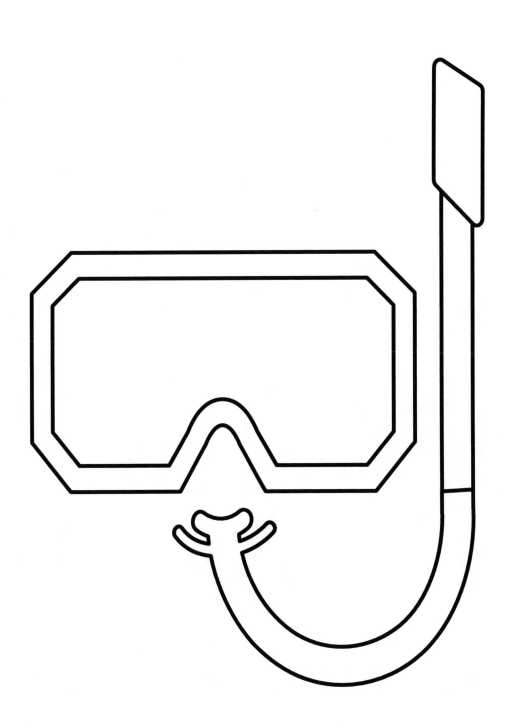

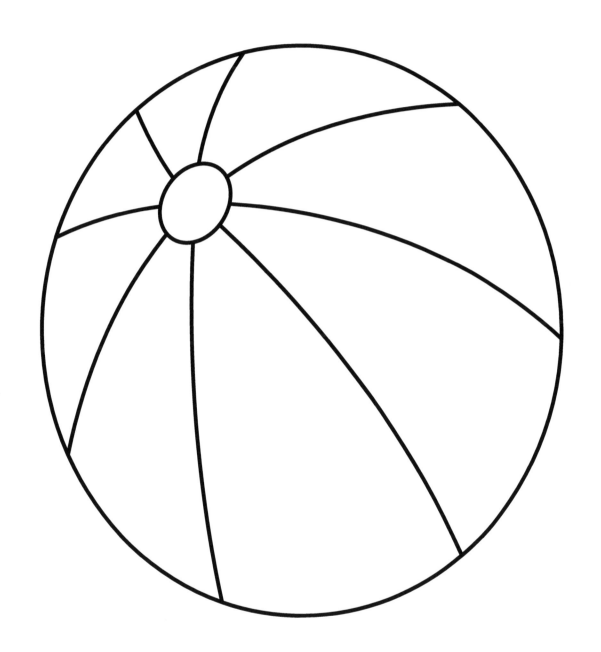

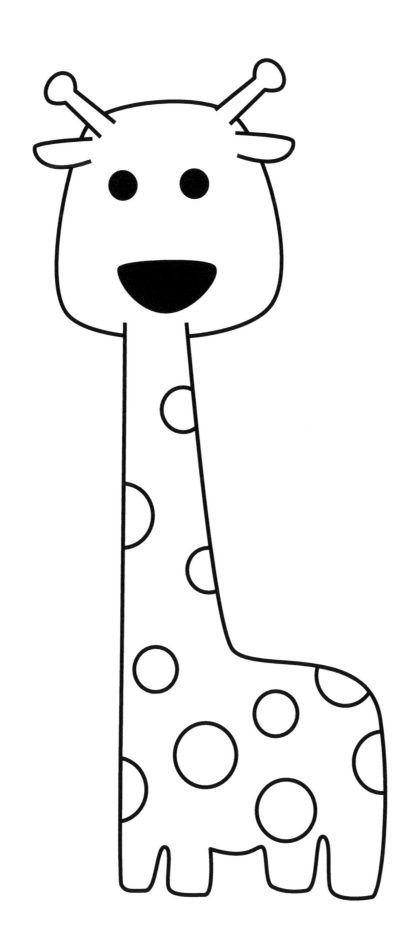

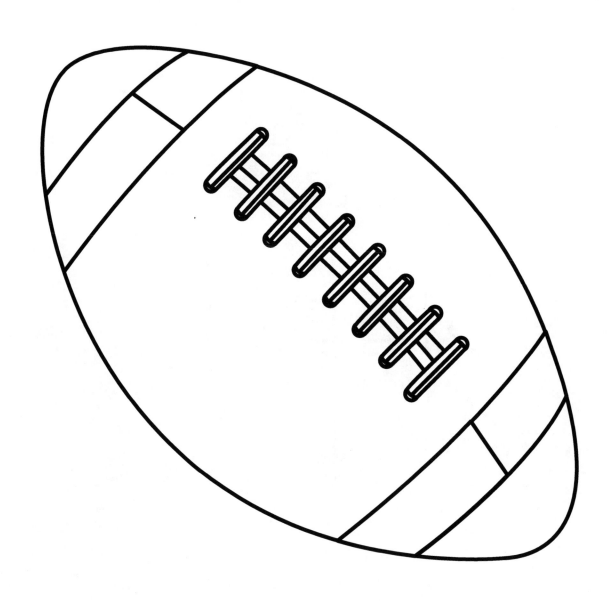

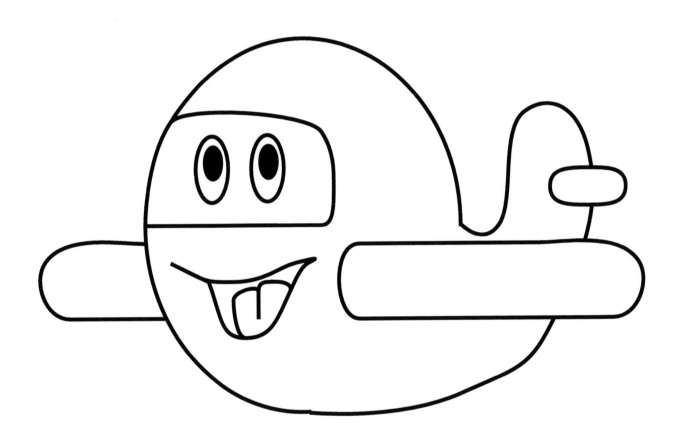

Made in United States
Troutdale, OR
11/25/2023